CHRISTMAS
A.B.C

Blushing Rose Publishing

Designed by Roni Akmon

Compiled By Nancy Akmon

Efforts have been made to find the copyright holders
of material used in this publication. We apologize for
any omissions or errors and will be pleased to include
the appropriate acknowledgements in future editions.

ISBN# 1-884807-42-9

Blushing Rose Publishing
P.O. Box 2238
San Anselmo, Ca. 94979
www.blushingrose.com

Printed and Bound in China

A Christmas Alphabet

A is for Apple that hangs on the tree,

B is for Bells that chime out in glee.

C is for Candy to please boys and girls

D is for Dolly with long flaxen curls.

E is for Evergreens decking the room.

F is for Flowers
of sweetest
perfume.

G is for Gifts
that bring us delight,

H is for Holly with red berries bright.

I is for Ice, so
shining and clear

J is the Jingle
of bells far and near

K is Kris
Kringle

with fur cap
and coat

L is for Letters the children all wrote.

M is for Mistletoe shining like wax

N is for Nuts which grandpapa cracks

O is for Oranges yellow and sweet

P is Plum Pudding a holiday treat.

Q the Quadrille in
which each one must dance.

R for the Reindeer that
gallop and prance.

T is for Turkey
so tender and brown.

S is for Snow that
falls silently down.

U is for Uproar
that goes on all day.

V is for Voices
that carol away.

Y is for Yule-log that burns clear and bright.

W for Wreaths hung up on the wall.

Z is for Zest shown from morning till night

X is for Xmas with pleasures for all.

Kriss Kringle reading the letters from the children.

Here are Kriss Kringle's Brownies at work on the toys, that are going to bring pleasure to good girls and boys . They busily labor from morning till night, and their smiles show quite plainly the work's a delight. For, like Kriss, they love children, and gladly assist in pleasing the thousands he has on his list.

This Brownie is showing some toys he's designed to Kriss,
To find out if they're just to his mind: By his eyes' merry twinkle I think we can tell
that in Kriss' opinion they'll do very well.

Starting off with sleigh full of toys on the Christmas Eve Journey.

On the roof of the house see Kriss Kringle;
He has climbed to the tall chimney-top,
And speedily down to the bottom
Both he and his bundle will drop.
Not in the least does it matter
How narrow the passage may be,
To find his way through he will manage,
So nimble and clever is he.

"Well, I've got down all right! Now for the stockings!"

A Visit From St. Nicholas

Twas the night before Christmas, when all through the house-Not a creature was stirring, not even a mouse; The stockings were hung by the chimney with care, in hopes that St. Nicholas soon would be there; The children were nestled all snug in their beds, While visions of sugar-plums danced in their heads; And Mama in her kerchief, and I in my cap, Had just settled our brains for a long winter's nap. When out on the lawn there arose such a clatter, I sprang from my bed to see what was the matter.

Away to the window I
flew like a flash,
Tore open the shutters,
and threw up the sash.
The moon, on the
breast of the new
fallen snow, gave the
luster of midday
objects below; When
what to my wondering
eyes should appear, But
a miniature sleigh and
eight tiny reindeer,
With a little old driver,
so lively and quick,
I knew in a moment it
must be St. Nick.
More rapid than eagles
his coursers they came,
And he whistled, and
shouted, and called
them by name:
"Now Dasher!
Now Dancer!
Now Prancer and
Vixen! On, Comet! On
Cupid! On Donner and
Blitzen! To the top of
the Porch! To the top
of the wall! Now dash
away! Dash away!
Dash away all!"
As dry leaves that
before the wild
hurricane fly,

When they meet with an obstacle, mount to the sky; So up to the house-top the coursers they flew- With the sleigh full of toys, and St. Nicholas too. And then, in a twinkling, I heard on the roof The prancing and pawing of each little hoof- As I drew my head, and was turning around, Down the chimney St. Nicholas came with a bound. He was dressed all in fur, from his head to his foot, And his clothes were all tarnished with ashes and soot; A bundle of toys he had flung on his back, and he looked like a peddler just opening his pack. His eyes- how they twinkled; his dimples, how merry! His cheeks were like roses, his nose like a cherry ! His droll little mouth was drawn up like a bow, And the beard of his chin was as white as snow;

The stump of a pipe he held tight in his teeth, and the smoke it encircled his head like a wreath; He had a broad face and a little round belly- That shook, when he laughed, like a bowl full of jelly. He was chubby and plump, a right old elf, And I laughed when I saw him, in spite of myself; A wink of his eye and a twist of his head- Soon gave me to know I had nothing to dread; He spoke not a word, but went straight to his work, And filled all the stockings; then turned with a jerk, And laying his finger aside of his nose, And giving a nod, up the chimney he rose; He sprang to his sleigh, to his team gave a whistle, And away they all flew like the down of a thistle. But I heard him exclaim, ere he drove out of sight, "Happy Christmas to all, and to all a good night!"

Clement Clark Moore
1823